Everything
You Need to
Know About

School
Violence

Violence is increasing every-where, even in schools.

Everything You Need to Know About

School Violence

Anna Kreiner

The Rosen Publishing Group, Inc.
New York

Published in 1996, 2000 by The Rosen Publishing Group, Inc.
29 East 21st Street, New York, NY 10010

Revised Edition, 2000

Library of Congress Cataloging-in-Publication Data

Kreiner, Anna
    Everything you need to know about school violence / Anna Kreiner
      p. cm — (The need to know library)
    Includes bibliographical references and index.
    Summary: A thoughtful discussion of violence in schools, complete
with examples of incidents and suggestions for coping.
    ISBN 0-8239-3304-0
    1. School violence—United States—Juvenile literature. 2. School
management and organization—United States—Juvenile literature.
[1. Violence. 2. Schools. 3. Weapons—Safety measures.
4. Safety] I. Title II. Series
I. Title. II. Series.
LB3013.3K74 1995
371.5'8—dc2O

                           94-24121
                              CIP
                              AC

Printed in the United States of America.

Contents

Graffiti is a fairly common form of violence.

Introduction: When Schools Aren't Safe

*J*anelle and Max are watching television. A special news bulletin interrupts their program. An announcer comes on and says, "There has been another high school shooting. Four students and one teacher are reported dead and several more have been seriously injured. Police have two students in custody as the suspected gunmen. They are described as a fifteen-year-old male and a seventeen-year-old male. Both are students at the high school. The motive for the shooting is as yet unknown."

Janelle angrily turns off the television.

"I can't believe this has happened again!" Max says in shock.

Learning about teen violence and murders has long-lasting effects on everyone.

"I'm afraid to go to school," says Janelle. "What if someone starts shooting at us in class?"

"This is really frightening," Max agrees. "When is it going to end?"

Violence: A Growing Problem in Schools

In the last couple of years, there has been a terrifying increase in episodes of school violence and related deaths. This was highlighted in April 1999 by the tragic shootings at Columbine High in Littleton, Colorado, in which two troubled students opened fire on their class-mates and the faculty. Twelve students and one teacher were killed before the gunmen committed suicide. No one knows for sure why incidents like this are on the rise.

Violence is defined as the use of force to cause damage or injury. School violence ranges from mild crimes such as spraying graffiti, to more serious crimes like destroying expensive school equipment and making threats against students and teachers. The most serious school violence of all occurs when actual physical harm is inflicted on students and teachers. Students bringing knives and guns into schools with the specific intent of doing harm has resulted in some of the worst outbreaks of school violence in history.

School is a place for learning and for developing your social skills. It should be a safe environment for everyone. So why has there been an increase in school violence? What are the causes of violence in schools? Can anything be done to prevent it? How can you stay safe in an atmosphere that is becoming more and more dangerous? This book will answer these questions and others. In addition, it will help you understand why violence occurs in schools and offer you resources, suggestions, and, most important hope.

The Columbine tragedy increased the nation's awareness of school violence.

Chapter One | School Violence: A Continuing Problem

April 20, 1999—Littleton, Colorado. 11:15 AM. Two students casually walk into Columbine High School. They fire several rounds from an arsenal of guns at their classmates. Then they place homemade bombs around the school. When it is all over, fourteen students, including the gunmen, and one teacher are dead. Many others are injured.

The news of the Columbine shootings shocked not only the Littleton community but also the entire country. The tragedy magnified the growing problem of school violence nationwide. The victims of the shootings were people who had interests and aspirations similar to those of your fellow classmates and teachers.

11

In one instant, however, violence had taken their lives and instilled such a sense of fear and loss that it will take time for survivors, family, and friends to heal.

In the last couple of years, news like this has made headlines all too often. But why? What is happening to these teens to make them so angry that they feel the need to hurt or kill? There are many possible reasons, such as bad grades, peer pressure, and problems at home, that may explain why teens turn to violence as a way of venting their frustrations.

The Increase in Crime in Our Schools

The use of weapons is definitely on the rise in the United States. Despite public support for gun control, access to guns is relatively easy. An increasing number of students carry guns and other types of weapons, such as box cutters, to school. Many teachers and students now believe that their schools are unsafe.

According to a Bureau of Justice Statistics report entitled "Indicators of School Crime and Safety, 1999":

- Students ages twelve through eighteen were the victims of about 1.1 million nonfatal, serious violent crimes at school.

- At the middle and high school levels, physical attacks or fights—without a weapon—were generally the most commonly reported crime during the 1996-97 school year.

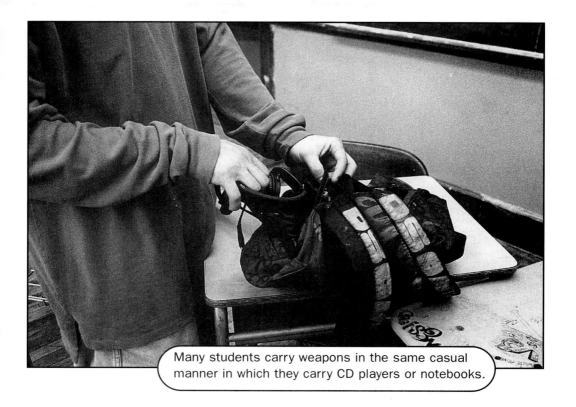

Many students carry weapons in the same casual manner in which they carry CD players or notebooks.

- In 1997, 18 percent of students reported carrying a weapon at some time in the past thirty days.

- In 1997, about 7 to 8 percent of students reported being threatened with a weapon such as a gun, knife, or club on school property within the last twelve months.

- Between 1993 and 1997, teachers were the victims of 1.8 million nonfatal crimes at school, including 1.1 million thefts and 657,000 violent crimes.

- In 1997, about one-third of all students in grades nine through twelve said that someone stole or deliberately damaged their property,

Violence is found everywhere, even in lyrics of popular songs.

such as their car, clothing, or books, while they were at school.

These statistics demonstrate that school violence has become increasingly commonplace. Students and teachers are all too commonly hit, stabbed, kicked, or shot. Sometimes a single student is the attacker, while at other times groups of students gang up on a teacher or another student. In one urban school district in New York, nearly 100 teachers have been assaulted by students each year for the past four years.

Although most of the aggressors are male, female students also carry weapons and act out physically.

As a result, more than three-quarters of American

teenagers believe that threats of violence are a problem in their schools.

And recently more than 80 percent of the nation's school districts reported that violent crime had increased during the past five years.

Is School Safe?

"Give me your money or else." This might sound like a scene from a back alley. But unfortunately, the speaker was a junior high school student in Wisconsin. It is not an isolated case. Almost 40 percent of the nation's eighth-graders have been threatened with violence. And almost one out of five has been injured at school.

Schools should be a safe place for learning. When someone is afraid, he or she is not able to learn as well. Fear reduces that person's ability to concentrate completely on school and be a good student. Unfortunately, more than one-third of the students polled in a recent survey said they were afraid at school.

At one school, a nineteen-year-old female student struck the principal over the head with a bottle of soda. In another case of school violence, a seventeen-year-old student was charged with trying to rape a fifteen-year-old in a classroom after school.

You probably have become familiar with names like Columbine, West Paducah, and Jonesboro—scenes of the worse incidents of school violence. In highly publicized tragedies such as these, thirty-eight students and teachers died and sixty-three were injured in school shootings. The gunmen were students as young as eleven years old.

Because of shootings like these, students are afraid. Parents and teachers are afraid, too. The National Rifle Association (NRA) polled parents on what they thought about gun violence. Almost one-third of the adults said that they worry about gun violence when they send their children to school.

Violence also makes it harder for teachers to do a good job. They have to spend more time disciplining students. They may be distracted from their teaching if they fear for their safety. Some teachers have even given up teaching because they were afraid of violence in their schools.

Many people used to think that school violence was a problem only in city schools. During the 1970s, for example, teachers in urban schools were nine times more likely to be attacked than teachers in rural schools. In a large city, you are more likely to hear about crime and violence in the news every day. However, cities are not the only places where violence occurs. Violent crime also occurs in suburbs and rural towns. It happens everywhere—in public and private schools, in predominantly white schools and minority schools, in affluent suburbs and inner cities. The criminals in these cases are troubled children, teens, and adults. The victims are usually students and teachers caught in the crossfire.

Sometimes what you wear or carry can trigger a violent reaction in someone else.

School Violence in the Past

Kids have always broken the rules in school. Most of the "bad apples" caused trouble by talking out of turn or being late for class. They were discourteous or disruptive. But they were not usually violent.

But even a long time ago, students were causing serious problems. During the 1800s, educators and lawmakers began to recognize that juveniles do commit crimes. So they set up special juvenile courts and reform schools to try to help them mend their ways. Sometimes the reform schools worked, but more often they just kept the juveniles off the streets until they became adult criminals.

In the twentieth century, legislators, teachers, and the public have had different opinions about school discipline

17

and violence. In some cases, teachers have emphasized "progressive education," which encourages a relaxation of strict discipline. If they thought students were getting away with too much, they tried to reimpose stricter standards.

The 1950s and 1960s saw many changes in society. People began to question authority, particularly when it seemed racist or sexist. Students stood up for their rights in a way they had not done before. Many young people liked these social changes. They didn't have to submit to the rules and strict disciplinary policies of the past that many thought were unfair.

But some people think that the relaxation in school discipline was a mistake. They blame the current rise in school violence on lax rules. If students think they can get away with violence, these people argue, then they will act out. These people believe that public schools should have strict regulations and be allowed to expel troublemakers. They believe that the schools are the problem.

Many private schools have high standards that public school teachers envy. "Students in the private schools realize that if they don't live up to the standard of the school, they will have to leave," said one public school teacher.

School Violence Today

Since the late 1970s, there has been a steady rise in

school violence. But incidents have been more frequent in the last few years.

Here are some recent news items involving crime and schools:

- February 2, 1996. Moses Lake, Washington. A fourteen-year-old student uses a hunting rifle to gun down an algebra teacher and three students at his junior high school. The young killer is convicted of two counts of aggravated first-degree murder and is sentenced to two life terms without parole.

- October 1, 1997. Pearl, Mississippi. A sixteen-year-old boy stabs his mother to death, then goes to Pearl High School and shoots nine students. Two are killed and seven are wounded. The shooter is convicted as an adult and is now serving three life sentences.

- May 19, 1998. Fayetteville, Tennessee. An eighteen-year-old honor student shoots a classmate to death in the school's parking lot. The motive: The victim was dating the honor student's ex-girlfriend.

- June 15, 1998. Richmond, Virginia. A fourteen-year-old student, angry with a classmate, opens fire in a crowded high school hallway. A social studies teacher and a volunteer are wounded. The student pleads guilty to five charges and will remain at a school for troubled boys until he completes his program.

- May 1999. President Clinton comments on a shooting several days past in Conyers, Georgia, in which six students were injured. He states that this incident is "as deeply troubling to me as it is to all Americans."

Chapter Two

What Are the Causes of School Violence?

The biggest question on everyone's mind regarding school violence is why is this happening—why are kids becoming violent? The National Center for Victims of Violent Crime says that during the 1996-97 school year, one in ten U.S. public schools reported experiencing at least one serious violent crime.

Although the national crime rate is on the decline, we still live in a violent society. According to a 1998 Bureau of Justice Statistics survey, Americans age twelve or older experienced approximately 31 million violent and property crimes. Teenagers are constantly reminded of shootings and murders in the news. Violence is also evident in many movies, television programs, music, and video games that entertain kids.

The gates of the schoolyard can't keep these problems

out. So it is not surprising that many teachers and students experience violence in the classroom.

Gangs and Drugs

Jeff knew he had made a mistake. He had worn a red sweatshirt to school. Red was the color of one of the gangs at school. Now they would be out to get him, assuming he was baiting them. Jeff put his knife in his pocket. He hoped he wouldn't have to use it, but he was ready.

It's easy to get involved in gangs. Selling drugs and making big money can be tempting, especially when you need money fast. Joining a gang may also seem like a good way to belong. Gang life may seem glamorous and exciting from the outside, but it is very dangerous.

"I have to carry a gun," said one student in a Los Angeles school where gang violence is common. "If I don't have a weapon, how can I protect myself from another guy who does have one?"

Almost all gang members have either been the victim of violence or know someone who has. Many innocent bystanders have been victims as well.

Drug use by teens can also result in more violence at school. Someone who is high on drugs is more likely to behave impulsively, take risks, be angry, or hurt someone. A drug addict may also steal from other students or teachers to pay for his habit.

Abuse at Home: The Seed for Potential Violence

Many young people learn early in life that violence is acceptable. Our society, and sometimes our families, accept violence—and sometimes even promote it.

Children who grow up in homes where there is domestic abuse think violence is a normal part of life. Many violent people were abused when they were young. Young people who are abused or who see other family members abused often lash out themselves. They become violent because they are angry. Sometimes they use their fists because they don't know any other way to solve their problems.

"I didn't know my dad shouldn't hit my mom," said one young woman. "I thought that was how everyone acted."

One teen was sentenced to four years in a juvenile detention center after he brutally attacked a younger classmate. "That's how my stepdad got us to do what he wanted," he said from his cell. "I figured the same way would work for me."

The Changing Family

Some people believe that the rise in the number of single-parent families has led to an increase in school violence. They think that parents either don't have the energy or the desire to teach values to their kids.

Parents are working longer hours, and more teens face the responsibilities of being alone.

But not everyone agrees with that view. "My mom taught me the difference between right and wrong," says a boy who grew up in a crime-ridden section of Los Angeles. "It was important to her, so she made time to do it."

Other people think that the breakdown of the family has led to violence by creating greater stress on parents and children. Many parents work long hours. They have little time to spend with their families. Often, kids return to an empty home after school while the parents are still at work. Some teens become the caretakers of their younger siblings. The extra responsibility can be overwhelming, leading teens to feel lonely, frustrated, and angry. Others feel unloved or unsupported because

According to a study by the federal government, one in twenty students carries a gun.

their parents are too busy to pay attention to them. Some of them join gangs for friendship and excitement. Others become angry loners and may use violence against the people around them.

Could You Get a Gun?

How easy is it for students to get guns? Could you get one if you wanted to? Most people usually think about firearms in the hands of kids living in urban areas. However, they are not the only ones with access to guns.

"My dad has a gun collection," says Julie, a student in an affluent Chicago suburb. "In fact, several relatives of mine have guns. My dad keeps his guns in the base-ment. The key to the safe is on my dad's key ring. So if

I wanted to get a gun out of there, it would be pretty easy to do. I'd just wait until my dad was asleep."

Private citizens like Julie's father own over 200 million guns. A Florida School Boards Association and the Association of School Administrators survey found that nearly 93 percent of the weapons brought to school came from the students' homes or from friends' or relatives' homes. According to a National Parents' Resource Institute for Drug Education survey, nearly one in thirteen high school students carries a gun to school. In the survey, thirty-five students had threatened to use a gun to harm another student or a teacher.

Another survey found that almost one-quarter of the students responding had taken a weapon to school during the past month. They carried the weapon either to protect themselves or to use in a fight.

The widespread violence and crime in America contribute to the violence in our schools. But just as important as the occurrence of violence is our attitude toward it.

Weapons for Self-Protection

Occurrences of school violence can sometimes lead to more violence in the future. Once violence has occurred, students get scared and want to protect themselves. They bring weapons to school for protection. Suddenly everyone starts to arm themselves for self-defense. "I have actually thought about bringing one of my dad's guns to school with me," says Julie. "I mean, I already know kids that bring guns to school. So why should I leave myself unprotected? I have to defend myself in any way I can."

Violence and the Media: Don't Try This at Home

Fifteen-year-old Jared loved action movies. Ever since he was young, he always enjoyed watching high-speed car chases, seeing guns going off, bombs ripping through buildings, and bad guys being blown to pieces. In most of these movies, the good guys won, though they usually used violence to solve a problem. It was thrilling to Jared.

Jared was partying with a few other kids at his best friend Howie's house. Howie's parents were away for the weekend, so the kids had the house to themselves. They played loud music and drank alcohol. Most of them were drunk and were having a good time.

Jared and Howie were in Howie's parents' bedroom looking around. They were buzzed. "Look at this," Howie said, pulling a gun from his father's nightstand. "I look like that bad guy from that awesome movie we saw yesterday." Jared didn't think much about it since he knew Howie was just

Movies, television, and radio frequently blur the distinction between violence and entertainment.

pretending. Howie was waving the gun, laughing. "Watch this," he said as he aimed the gun at his own head and pulled the trigger. A shot was fired. Before Jared could do anything, Howie lay dead on the floor. Blood was splattered everywhere. Howie forgot to check to see if the gun was actually loaded. Jared was stunned to see real violence up close. It was totally different from those movies and television shows.

Violence in entertainment has been popular as long as entertainment itself has been around. However, the entertainment industry has been widely criticized for sending the message to kids that violence is glamorous, fun, and exciting. Some kids cannot tell the difference between fantasy violence and real violence, so they misinterpret movies, television programs, and music that contains violence. They come away believing that violence can solve any problem.

But the media is not solely responsible for all of the violence in society. Society and the media feed off of one another. If people didn't like to see violence, then less of it would be shown. Recently the entertainment industry agreed to limit the amount of violence shown on television and in the movies. There are ratings systems that help parents decide what children can see or hear. Many young people, however, are still getting the message that there is a place for violence in our society.

Chapter Three | Getting Tough at School

Beep, beep, beep. Steve walked through the front door of his high school. He heard what sounded like a siren. Then he knew: It was a metal detector.

The school guard walked over. "Empty your pockets," he said.

Reaching into his backpack, Steve grabbed the knife and raised it to the guard's face. He wasn't going to give in without a fight.

The guard quickly knocked the knife out of Steve's hand. He called the police on his walkie-talkie. Within five minutes, a policeman arrived. He read Steve his rights. Steve was under arrest.

You can't necessarily tell which students are armed in school.

Weapons in School

You have probably walked through a metal detector in an airport or a federal office building. But some students now encounter them on a regular basis—in their schools. More schools are installing metal detectors and hiring security guards. Almost 15 percent of the nation's school districts use metal detectors. If a metal detector reveals that a student is carrying a weapon, serious action is taken. The weapon is confiscated and the authorities are contacted. Since the recent rash of school violence, strict punishments have been imposed on students caught with weapons.

Because of the rise in gun violence in the nation, the federal government and some states have passed strict weapons laws making the punishment for illegally carrying a gun much stiffer. In most states, it is illegal for anyone to sell a gun to a person under eighteen. In 1994, President Clinton signed the Gun-Free Schools Act. Under this law, a student caught possessing a weapon in school is expelled for one calendar year. Most schools today have zero tolerance policies, which are regulations that punish students severely no matter how minor the offenses are. Zero tolerance policies are aimed against students who cause school disruptions. These policies not only apply to weapons but also to fighting, gang activity, and drugs.

This Is Not a Game

At lunch one day, Todd told Kenny in a hushed voice to look in his bag. It contained a gun. "I'm going to use it on Mr. Washington," Todd whispered. "He has been so hard on me. He's gonna get what's coming to him!" After lunch Kenny went straight to the principal's office and told the principal about Todd's gun. The principal and security guards immediately went and opened Todd's locker and found the bag with the gun inside. Todd's punishment was swift and severe. He is now confined to a detention center for teenage boys.

Many teachers complain that student misbehavior interferes with teaching. They want stricter and better enforced rules in their schools. Some school districts have responded by imposing new disciplinary procedures. Students who commit violent acts may be suspended or expelled. In some states, juvenile delinquents are sent to prison camps, detention centers, or alternative schools.

Some reform schools help students who have behavior problems learn new ways of coping. But critics claim that many alternative schools are discriminatory "dumping grounds." They say that minority students are overrepresented and that the schools don't help the students at all. Then there are the districts that cannot afford alternative schools. Violent students from these areas either stay in the system or drop out.

Charles was new to Santa Monica High School. He didn't have many friends. Some of the students were afraid of him. He always seemed angry and frequently spoke about his dad's gun collection.

One day during lunch period, Charles started hitting his classmate Mark for no reason. It took two teachers to separate the boys. Charles injured the boy so badly that he had to be taken to the hospital.

Charles was arrested. The school later discovered that he had been previously arrested and expelled from his old school because of his violent behavior.

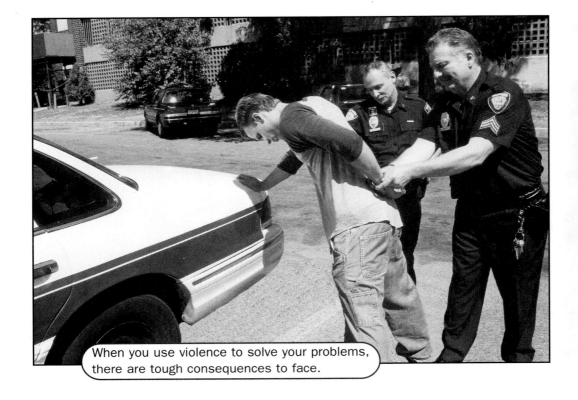

When you use violence to solve your problems, there are tough consequences to face.

The teachers were very upset. They hadn't known about Charles's record because, according to state laws, juvenile court records must be kept secret.

Students' Rights and the Get-Tough Attitude

Teachers are worried about their safety and want more information about violent students. In many states, the records of juvenile offenders are sealed. The court system protects the rights of young people by keeping this information private.

Teachers argue that they have a right to know about students who are prone to violence. In 1989, California adopted legislation requiring school districts in the state to inform teachers about students who had hurt or tried to hurt another person. The American Federation of Teachers, the nation's second largest teachers' union, wants access to more information. It believes that violence can be diminished if students who might act out are identified early and receive special attention.

Some schools are trying to reduce gang-related violence by prohibiting students from wearing clothes that are often associated with gangs—for instance, certain types of hats, pants, sneakers, sweatshirts, and jogging suits—to school. Since fights sometimes break out because a gang member thinks another student is wearing the "wrong" clothing, many teachers and students think this is a good policy.

Others believe a dress policy does not go to the heart of the problem, since gang-related violence makes up only a small part of the crime in most schools. They also think such rules unfairly restrict students' freedom of expression.

Many teachers and students approve of a stricter atmosphere in their schools. "It's time for someone to teach these kids a lesson," said one California teacher. "We've got to get back the discipline that has gone out the window."

"I feel safer knowing someone is looking out for us," says a student at a Maryland junior high where metal detectors were recently installed. But other people oppose the use of metal detectors and security checks. They believe that these methods violate students' rights.

In Detroit, the American Civil Liberties Union and the school district worked out a compromise. The district agreed to tell students before they installed metal detectors and to use them only where there was a problem with guns.

Teachers want parents to become more involved in the schools. In some districts, parents have joined the "get-tough" movement; they patrol school hallways looking for weapons and violent behavior.

Some educators believe that parents need to take a more active role at home, too. They want parents to teach self-discipline to their children and support the school's disciplinary procedures.

Many people think the get-tough attitude helps. They believe students use violence simply because they think they can get away with it.

How Can This Violence Be Stopped?

Metal detectors and stricter police protection can help to reduce violence. But some students still take weapons to school. They learn how to hide their guns, knives, and box cutters. And students will always have at least one weapon—their fists.

A more important part of solving the problem is to help students recognize that violence is unacceptable.

They need to realize that it will not solve their problems and that its consequences can be very serious for their victims and for themselves.

As long as students think violence will help them get what they want, they will continue to hurt other people and property. By challenging students to reconsider their attitudes toward violence, schools and parents can help to make long-lasting changes.

Sometimes people use violence because they feel overwhelmed by their problems. Some are angry at themselves and the world around them. Students, parents, and teachers should keep an eye on troubled students and report any odd or threatening behavior. Even something that appears to be small or insignificant may actually be a very loud cry for help. Be aware of the people around you. It can make a world of difference.

The next chapter discusses how schools are trying to change the way students think about violence and help the students manage their problems in other, more productive ways.

Chapter Four | **Changing How We Think About Violence**

*T*he students stand in front of the judge.

Yesterday the two boys were arguing about money. Each one claimed the other had stolen $10 from his locker.

They began to scuffle in the schoolyard. Before they became violent, the teacher on duty broke up the fight. Then she told them they would have to see the judge.

But this judge isn't wearing a long robe. She's not sitting in a courtroom. The judge is another student and "court" is being held in a school classroom.

Peer Mediation

Many schools have introduced peer mediation to reduce

violence in their classrooms. In the previous example, a school set up a mock court in class where arguments can be settled as if in a real courtroom. These programs help students resolve conflicts before they become violent. The mediators are students who have been trained to listen carefully and offer fair solutions. Each student presents his or her side of the story. Then the mediator or mediation team draws up an agreement for both sides to sign.

Getting Extra Help

Schools used to be places to learn the three R's—reading, writing, and arithmetic. But now many are adding a fourth R: relationships. Most violence occurs between people who know each other, not strangers. So it is important to learn how to talk to the people you know and solve your problems with them without using violence.

For teachers in 1940, the most serious student problems were talking out of turn, chewing gum in class, and making noise. But today's students present more serious problems. In the 1990s, teachers listed violence in the schools as their number one education-related concern. Physical conflicts and weapon possession were at the top of teachers' lists of concerns.

Educators know that students face many challenges outside of school. When you are worried about gangs, drugs, and alcohol in your neighborhood, it can be hard to feel safe anywhere. Sometimes students take out their anger and frustration on the people around them.

Counselors and teachers want to prevent violence before it happens. They teach students nonviolent methods for reducing stress and dealing with anger.

"I used to use my fists when I got angry," says one student who has been suspended four times for violent behavior. "Now I'm learning to talk about what bothers me." At a school clinic in Alabama, students can get extra help to cope with drug and alcohol problems and family stress. Local businesses, churches, and community centers are also trying to help young people find alternatives to gangs, drugs, and fighting. "I ran with a gang because there was nothing else to do," says one youth at a community center in Milwaukee. "Now I know that at least one night a week I can come here to play basketball and have some fun."

Forming Relationships

There is another important reason why focusing on relationships can help to reduce violence: many criminals feel no connection to other people in their lives. They look at other people almost as objects. They forget that the person at the other end of the knife blade or gun barrel is just like them in many important ways.

Researchers have found that adolescent murderers tend to be not just violent, but extremely violent. One

Drug and alcohol abuse among teens is rising. It is likely that this is contributing to the rise in violent behavior.

teenage murderer stabbed his victim forty-six times.

A psychologist who studies violent teens believes that these young people feel very bad about themselves. "For a person to treat his or her victim like a piece of meat—I believe you yourself have to have been dehumanized."

These violent teens often do not care what they do to themselves or to anyone else. When you feel good about yourself, you are less likely to use violence.

Who Suffers the Consequences of Violent Behavior?

Schools are also helping students to consider the direct effects of violent behavior. For example, former gang members in Los Angeles and other cities talk to students about gang life. "Yeah, it's cool and exciting," says one former gang member, "and you can make money. But that's only good if you're alive." Almost all gang members have been involved in violent activity by the time they've been in the gang for four years. Former gang members know that it's not a good idea to bet on getting out before the violence starts. "You never know when the guy in the next car will pull out an Uzi. It could be tonight."

But gang-related and drug-related violence are only part of the problem of school violence. A student is more likely to be shot by another student during a feud

There are several people you can turn to if you have a problem with drugs or alcohol.

Getting a part-time job will not only give you a sense of responsibility and a place to belong, but it will teach you valuable skills.

about a boyfriend or girlfriend or a disagreement over possessions than to be shot by a gang member.

Many of the students who were arrested after their school shooting rampages are now serving life sentences behind bars, where there is no future. Other students are beginning to realize the serious consequences of their violent behavior. These students will spend the rest of their lives in jail, thinking about the harm and pain inflicted on their victims and their families.

But remember, violence can be prevented. A reform school in Boston is trying to help violent youths develop better problem-solving skills. They are learning to think of alternatives to violence.

The teachers ask the students the following question: Another kid has the last ball on the field. You want to play with it. What do you do? The first reaction of many students? Hit the other student and take the ball. After going through a special problem-solving program, more students came up with a new answer: play catch.

Students are also learning how dangerous weapons can be. This type of education has to start early. Most weapons-related crime occurs in high school, but almost one-quarter of the gun-related violence takes place in junior high.

A New Outlook on Life

Another way schools are trying to reduce the violence is by giving students hope.

"What difference does it make?" said a teen living in a high-crime area of a large city. "If I don't shoot them, they'll shoot me. And probably someone else will shoot both of us anyway."

Unfortunately for many youths, violence has become a way of life and death. They don't believe they have a future. They do not expect to get a job or live in a safe neighborhood. So they find it easier to go along with what's happening at the moment. Often they use violence to get what they want right away.

Schools try to help these students by giving them

skills they can use to get a good job. They also help them plan for a successful future. Here is a story of one person who chose life over violence:

Billy and Eddie had been friends since they were kids, but they started hanging out with different crowds in high school. Eddie became friends with a guy who was part of a local gang. He invited Eddie to join the gang. Billy tried to convince Eddie not to become a member but he didn't listen.

While Eddie was hanging out with his new friends, Billy started working at a local automotive parts store. During his breaks he would go out back and watch the guys work in the auto shop. Billy hoped to work on cars with them one day. He was researching different auto schools at the school library.

One day Eddie stopped by the shop to see Billy. He was telling Billy that he was trying to leave the gang because of the violence. "They say I can't leave," Eddie said. "Once I'm in, I'm in."

A month later, Eddie and Billy were walking down the street when a car drove by. Two shots rang out. Before Billy knew what had happened, Eddie lay bleeding on the sidewalk. Billy ran inside a store and called for an ambulance, but it was too late. Eddie later died from the gunshot wound inflicted by one of his fellow gang members.

Billy was lucky. He could have been shot, too. After that incident, Billy became a peer counselor at his neighborhood community center. He wanted to keep teens from choosing the same self-destructive path of violence that Eddie had followed.

You can also become a peer counselor in a community center like Billy. You can talk to teens who are confused or need help. Your mission is to help students stay in school, be safe, and avoid trouble. Most neighborhood community centers have teen programs. They provide many activities, from social events and chat sessions to outreach programs and work-related training. Community centers offer teens something to do and a safe place for them to hang out with their friends.

There are people who are working together to stop school violence. They are working to set up outreach programs, hotlines, memorials, support programs, and counseling programs for teens coping with violence. You can work to end school violence. The next chapter gives you some answers about how you can stay safe and help prevent violence.

Chapter Five | Staying Safe in School: What Can You Do?

You know that violence is a problem in many schools. Although knowing about a problem will not make it go away, once you are aware that it exists, you can figure out ways to keep the violence from spreading. The most important step is to learn how to protect yourself in a violent situation. But you can also help to achieve a larger goal: preventing violence before it happens.

Be On Your Guard!

How can you protect yourself?

First, listen to your instincts. If you feel unsafe or uncomfortable in an empty classroom, hallway, or in a particular section of the school grounds, pay attention! Try to leave or find an alternative route.

Pay attention to your surroundings. Is someone walking uncomfortably close behind you? Don't just

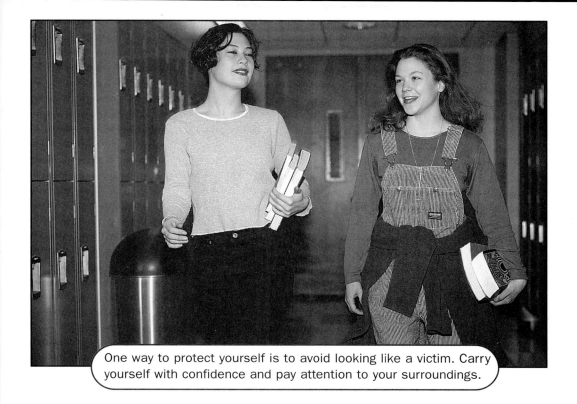

One way to protect yourself is to avoid looking like a victim. Carry yourself with confidence and pay attention to your surroundings.

pretend you don't notice—do something to increase the distance between you and that person. Are you in a crowded hallway? Then surround yourself with people, or turn abruptly to the side so that the stream of people will carry you away from the threatening person. What if someone follows you home? Go into a store and stay near the cash register. Tell the manager that you think someone may be following you.

If you see a student with a gun, knife, or other weapon, tell someone! Tell a teacher, the principal, your parents, a guidance counselor, or another adult. If you don't feel you can tell the adult in person, write a letter. You do not have to give your name.

You should not take a weapon away from another

One way to avoid potentially violent situations is to not use drugs.

student. It is best to let school officials or the police handle the situation. If you come across a gun or object that can inflict harm, bring it to the attention of school officials or a security guard immediately!

If someone threatens you with a weapon, it is usually best not to fight back. Do what the person orders, and then report the incident to the authorities.

Suppose you are in the schoolyard, and someone threatens you. "I'm gonna get you," he says. "I may not bring my gun to school, but there's nothing to stop me from using it later. Watch out." What should you do?

If anyone threatens you, tell a trusted adult right away. Just because you won't be on school property doesn't mean the school staff will be reluctant to help you. They can notify the police and your parents, who will help you to stay safe.

It is important to remember that violence does not require weapons. Try to avoid confrontations with students who might threaten you with violence. For instance, if you get angry with someone, do not use insults or name-calling. It might feel good at the moment, but you are likely to make the other person angry. If the two of you become involved in a physical fight, you may both get hurt.

It is important to talk about your anger. If you think you can have a reasonable conversation, tell the other person in a non-threatening way what he or she did and why you feel angry. If that does not seem possible, talk to an adult or a trusted friend. They may be able to help you deal with the other student. Even if you decide not to confront the person who made you angry, the person you tell can help you handle your anger constructively.

Do your best not to get involved in violent situations. If you can, walk away from anyone who threatens you, especially if the person has a weapon. If you cannot, stay calm and try to negotiate your way out of a potentially violent situation.

It is not a good idea to fight back, even in a fistfight. Walk away if you can. Do not use violence just to save your pride. Use physical force only when you cannot get away and you think you will be in greater danger if you don't fight back. One way to be prepared to fight back when the situation calls for it is by taking self-defense classes.

Never bring a weapon into school. Violence is more likely to happen if there is a weapon available. Even if you are just carrying your weapon for self-defense, you might end up using it if you get angry with someone. Without a weapon, you will have more time to think before you act. Too often, the weapon is used against its owner.

The Smart Way: Helping Yourself

If you think that you are likely to become violent, there are several steps you can take to help yourself. First of all, never carry a gun, knife, or other weapon. Second, stay away from gangs and drugs.

If you tend to use violence when you get angry or feel overwhelmed, talking to someone can help. If you don't want to talk to your parents, try a guidance counselor, an older brother or sister, or a friend. Youth leaders and clergypeople are also good listeners.

The person you talk to may not be able to solve your problem directly, but just knowing that someone cares about you can make you feel better. And that person may recommend other people who may be able to help you. Then you will be less likely to react to your problem in a way that will hurt someone.

Think before you act. Shoot-outs may look exciting in the movies, but after the scene is finished, the actors put away their fake guns and go home for the night. If you shoot someone with a real bullet, your story will not have a happy ending.

Will violence solve your problems? You might think that hurting a classmate who has been bugging you will get rid of the problem. But what about the next time someone irritates you? You can't use your fists to fix everything that is wrong. If you use violence, you are likely to cause more problems—for your victim and for yourself.

Stop Violence Before It Happens

You can help prevent violence before it happens. One way is to start changing how you look at guns and violence. Do not act impressed if someone shows you a weapon he or she has brought to school. Do not encourage your friends to use their fists when they get angry.

Do your friends like to hang out in places where there is a lot of violence? Suggest other things to do such as playing sports or listening to music. You and your friends might also choose not to watch violent movies or television programs.

You can help your friends when they get upset. Tell them you want to listen to their problems and help them. Discourage them from getting involved with gangs.

For example: You walk into science class in back of Manuel. Joseph sticks out his foot and trips Manuel.

53

You might join or start a support group or a group aimed toward finding ways to stop violence in your school.

Manuel glares at Joseph. Then you hear him say, "I'll meet you at 3:00 out back. You know what for." You know that Manuel and Joseph fight a lot. And they usually get violent. What should you do? Tell an adult that you think there will be a fight after school. Then the adult can take action.

But suppose you do not know ahead of time that there is going to be a fight. Then, as you are leaving school, you see a crowd in the schoolyard. Manuel and Joseph look angry. They are starting to throw punches. What should you do? Get an adult right away. Do not encourage them to keep fighting. A fight may be exciting, but it is excitement with a high price.

These are some things you can do by yourself. You can also work with other people to reduce school violence.

Working with Others

A nonviolent life does not have to be boring. Talk to school officials and people involved in community centers in your area. Maybe you can organize an afterschool club or recreation time.

Your community center might set aside time for you to play sports or have parties. If the staff members know that people in your school are interested in these activities, they will be more likely to help you get what you want.

Do you want to be a peer mediator? Talk to your principal or guidance counselor. One of them may be able to help you start a program.

Talk with your friends about how you can feel safer in school. You might organize an afterschool support group. Drugs, alcohol, and fights with a boyfriend or girlfriend are hard problems, but you can get support from people who are having the same experiences.

You can be a role model for younger students. Sometimes kids imitate their older friends or relatives. When you say no to violence, you are setting a good example for them.

You might want to become a mentor. Everyone needs someone to listen to them. You turned to a close friend or an adult when you had a problem; now you can do the same for your friends or relatives in the lower grades. If other students in your school are interested, you can form a "big brothers/big sisters" club.

You can show your "brothers" and "sisters" that there are better choices than violence. At the same time, you will help yourself. Being a good friend and mentor will make you feel better about yourself.

"I still miss Eddie," says Billy after Eddie's murder. "Man, we used to do everything together. Eddie wanted to get out of that gang and there was nothing I could do to help him. I can't bring Eddie back, but I hope that my work at the community center can keep other students safe from such violence."

It's Up to You

When school violence happens, it creates a scary atmosphere in which no one feels safe. For those directly affected, it can leave physical and emotional scars that will take time to heal. School-related violence can be prevented. You can do your part, too. Each of us can help.

It is important to get rid of weapons. Guns, knives, box cutters, and other weapons are dangerous. You have to change how you think about violence. Hurting other people or stealing from them does not solve your

Students who feel good about themselves don't need to use violent behavior.

problems. Violence is not glamorous. It may seem exciting, but the results are deadly.

Students who feel good about themselves and close to the people around them do not need to use violence. When you can look forward to a good future, you will not lash out with your fists or destroy school property.

Today students, teachers, parents, and community leaders are working together to wipe out school violence. Awareness, counseling, and involvement in school violence prevention programs are some of the ways you can combat this problem. You can help make our schools a safe and secure place in which everyone can learn.

Glossary

aggressor Person who attacks or threatens another person.

confiscate Take away property.

domestic abuse The use of violence or hurtful words by one family member against another.

mediators People who listen to both sides of an argument and help find a solution.

mentor A trusted counselor or guide.

nuclear family Mother, father, and children who live together in one household.

reform or alternative schools Schools for young people who have broken the law.

vandalism Purposely destroying or damaging property.

violence The use of physical force to cause harm.

weapons Guns, knives, pipes, or other items used to cause injury or damage.

zero tolerance A policy used by schools to discipline and punish students for violent offenses.

Where to
Go for Help

In the United States

Center for the Prevention of School Violence
20 Enterprise Street, Suite 2
Raleigh, NC 27607-7375
(800) 399-6054
Web site: http://www.ncsu.edu/cpsv

Center to Prevent Handgun Violence
1225 Eye Street NW, Suite 1100
Washington, DC 20005
(202) 289-7319
Web site: http://www.handguncontrol.org

National School Safety Center
141 Duesenberg Drive, Suite 11
Westlake Village, CA 91362
(805) 373-9977
Web site: http://www.nssc1.org

Safe Alternatives and Violence Education (SAVE)
San Jose Police Department
201 West Mission Street
San Jose, CA 95110
(408) 277-4133
Web site: http://www.sjpd.org

In Canada

Kids Help Phone
(800) 668-6868
Web site: http://kidshelp.sympatico.ca

National Crime Prevention Centre
Department of Justice
St. Andrew's Tower
284 Wellington Street
Ottawa, ON K1A 0H8
(613) 941-9306
http://www.crime-prevention.org

For Further Reading

Begun, Ruth W., and Frank J. Huml. *Ready-to-Use Violence Prevention Skills Lessons & Activities for Secondary Students.* Paramus, NJ: Center for Applied Research in Education, 1998.

Chaiet, Donna. *Staying Safe at School.* New York: Rosen Publishing Group, 1995.

Cobain, Bev, RNC. *When Nothing Matters Anymore: A Survival Guide for Depressed Teens.* Minneapolis, MN: Free Spirit Publishing, Inc., 1998.

Cox, Vic. *Guns, Violence & Teens.* Springfield, NJ: Enslow Publishers, Inc., 1997.

Goodwin, William. *Teen Violence.* San Diego, CA: Lucent Books, 1997.

Miller, Maryann. *Coping with Weapons and Violence*

at School and on Your Streets. New York: Rosen
Publishing Group, 1999.

Schleifer, Jay, and Ruth C. Rosen. *Everything You
Need to Know About Weapons in School and at
Home*. New York: Rosen Publishing Group, 1994.

Index

About the Author

Anna Kreiner was born and raised in the Philadelphia area and received a master's degree in public health from the University of California at Los Angeles. She works as a freelance writer.

Photo Credits

Cover photo by Michael Brandt. All interior shots by Yung Hee Chia except p. 8 by Ira Fox; p. 10 © Corbis International; p. 28 by Katherine Hsu; p. 41 by Les Mills and p. 50 by Michael Brandt.